Weekly Reader Children's Book Club presents

The Improbable Adventures of MARVELOUS O'HARA SOAPSTONE

Also by Zibby Oneal

War Work

The Improbable Adventures of MARVELOUS O'HARA SOAPSTONE

Zibby Oneal

Paul Galdone drew the pictures

THE VIKING PRESS   NEW YORK

For my parents,
Mary Elizabeth and Dewey Bisgard

1

Lemon and Iris Soapstone lived in an ordinary square white house. They raised pigs in the garden. Raising pigs was their hobby. Other years they had other hobbies. This year it was pigs.

The pigs lived in a sty at the back of the garden just to the left of Mr. Soapstone's rose bed. Occasionally a pig escaped and ate a rose. The pigs preferred the yellow roses.

Not everyone cared for Lemon and Iris's hobby. Their mother, Mrs. Soapstone, hated it. Mrs. Soapstone liked things to be proper. If they couldn't be proper, she liked them to be interesting. "Pigs are neither proper nor interesting," she said. "They add nothing whatsoever to our garden." Mrs. Soapstone pretended to herself that the pigs were pre-Columbian sculpture.

Another person who didn't like pigs was the Soapstones' neighbor, Mrs. Chew. "I can hear those pigs barking all night," she said. This was a ridiculous thing to say, of course, but Mrs. Chew said lots of ridiculous things. Lemon and Iris thought Mrs. Chew was crazy.

Lemon and Iris didn't worry much about what Mrs. Chew thought, but they *had* to worry about their mother. Every fourth Friday when their mother's sewing circle met to sew on the screen porch, Lemon and Iris had to move the pigs to the garage and lock them in for the afternoon. Besides moving the pigs in, they had to move the fertilizer and the rose dust and the Black Leaf 40 out. This was in case the pigs got hungry. A pig will try anything once.

One day when Lemon and Iris were hauling a bale of peat moss out of the garage, getting ready for the pigs, Iris said, "We should have kept on collecting perfume bottles. It was easier."

"It was easier, yes, but not as interesting," said Lemon.

"If Mother liked pigs, this hobby would be interesting *and* easy," Iris said.

"But *that* won't happen till butter flies."

Lemon was older than Iris. She understood more things. Iris, on the other hand, could play the recorder and stand on her toes.

Iris and Lemon's father, Mr. Soapstone, liked pigs. He thought collecting perfume bottles was a waste of time. Raising pigs had some point to it. In the evening before supper he talked to the pigs. He rubbed their ears. He tickled their noses with petunias. Sometimes he sang them his favorite song, which was "Martha."

One night before supper Mr. Soapstone was leaning on the sty feeding the pigs verbena leaves. "The trouble with these pigs," he said, "is that they aren't good enough."

Lemon and Iris looked at their pigs. They looked good enough to them.

"What we want," their father said, "is top quality champion prize pigs that will win ribbons at the County Fair."

"Why?" said Lemon.

"Because if you do a thing, you should do it right," Mr. Soapstone said. "No point raising a flock of pigs that never amount to a row of pins."

Lemon and Iris shrugged. They didn't mind the pigs they had, but they liked blue ribbons and newspaper clippings as well as the next person.

"Buy us some prize pigs, then," said Iris.

That evening at supper Mr. Soapstone said to his wife, "Tomorrow I'm taking the pigs away."

"And high time, too," said Mrs. Soapstone. "They cause ants."

"I'm taking them to a farm in the country."

"Which is the proper place for pigs," said Mrs. Soapstone.

9

"But you'll find a farmer who loves them, won't you?" Lemon asked.

"And be sure he feeds them every day?" said Iris.

"I have a farmer in mind," their father said, "who will trade me a champion sow for our six pigs."

"You mean we're not getting rid of pigs altogether?" Mrs. Soapstone said.

"From now on we will not use the word pig," Mr. Soapstone replied. "From now on we will say champion."

2

Early the next day Mr. Soapstone loaded the pigs into his car and drove away. Iris and Lemon stood on the curb and waved good-by.

"I'll miss them," Lemon said.

"Yes, but before you can say Jack Robinson we'll have a champion," Iris replied.

"Still, they were our first pigs. I kind of loved them."

Iris sat down on the curb with her chin in her hands. "Don't talk about it," she said.

After a while they set about cleaning the sty. They wanted it perfect for the champion. Lemon hosed the slops trough. Iris raked the dirt into attractive patterns. They set a bouquet of impatiens in a watering can beside the fence. Then they sat down in the shade to wait for the champion.

"I wonder how you know a champion when you see one," Lemon said.

"A champion has certain traits," said Iris. "A person can usually tell."

Lemon sucked a blade of grass. She knew Iris didn't know a champion pig from a French horn.

Mrs. Soapstone was dusting the screen porch. Lemon could see she was happy the pigs were gone. Mrs. Chew was standing on a ladder painting a cherry tree on the east wall of her house. Lemon thought of going over to look at it, but she didn't really want to talk to Mrs. Chew. Mrs. Chew usually said something crazy that confused Lemon.

"I'm getting sleepy," Iris said. "If he doesn't hurry up and get here, I'll probably doze off."

Lemon chewed the blade of grass. She watched Mrs. Chew painting round red spots on the cherry tree. Every year Mrs. Chew painted something new on her house. Last year she had painted a wisteria vine over the front door. In a way it made her house interesting.

All at once there was a loud honking in the driveway. Lemon jumped up. "He's here!" she cried.

Mr. Soapstone's car rolled by in the driveway. Lemon and Iris could see a pink snout resting on the dashboard.

"I see the champion's nose!" Iris shouted.

Mr. Soapstone came hurrying out of the garage. His straw hat was askew. He looked excited.

"She's a beauty!" he called. "Best pig in the county!"

Lemon and Iris ran to the car. In the front seat they saw a small white pig. "My! that certainly looks like a prize pig!" Iris said.

"Bet your boots she's a prize!" Mr. Soapstone cried. "I wouldn't be surprised if this was the best pig this county's seen in twenty years!"

Lemon looked at the pig. She seemed awfully small.

"She's a baby, of course. We'll have to fatten her up," Mr. Soapstone said.

The pig grunted gently. Her snout quivered.

"She's a purebred Chester White," said Mr. Soapstone.

"Is that her name?" Lemon hoped not.

"No. That's a brand of pig. She hasn't any name yet."

The little pig had small pointed ears. She was covered with fine white hair. The sun shining on her made her glisten.

Mr. Soapstone lifted her out of the car. He put her in Lemon's arms. The little pig snuggled down and closed her eyes, resting her head on Lemon's chest. Lemon held her breath. She looked down at the little pig. Right away she knew she loved her.

"I was thinking we'd name her Letitia after my friend who moved to Pittsburgh," Iris said.

Lemon rocked the pig in her arms. One ear twitched. The pig sighed. "No," Lemon said, "I think we ought to call her Marvelous."

"Marvelous!" said Iris. "That's no name."

"But that's what she is," said Lemon, rocking the pig.

"I think that's a darned fine name," said Mr. Soapstone. "That's just the right kind of name for a blue-ribbon champion."

"I think it's weird," said Iris. But all the same they decided they'd call the pig Marvelous.

3

Mr. Soapstone got out his hog book and looked up some things. "We have to feed her plenty," he said. "I want her to double her weight every two weeks."

Lemon and Iris filled the slops bucket. They carried it out to the sty and emptied it into the trough. Marvelous came over to the fence and looked at them. Lemon felt a little shy with the new pig. "Your lunch is ready," she said politely.

Marvelous wiggled her snout. She looked at Lemon through a fringe of white eyelashes. "I hope you'll like it," Lemon added.

Marvelous grunted. She nosed the slops trough. Lemon and Iris watched her. She didn't eat a bite.

"Maybe she doesn't like oatmeal," Lemon said.

"Probably she hates it," said Iris, who hated it.

They sat on the fence and watched. Marvelous took one more sniff at the slops trough. Then she grunted quietly and walked to the other side of the sty.

"Now that worries me," Lemon said. "I wonder if she isn't feeling well."

"Champions usually have small appetites," said Iris.

Lemon snorted. "You don't know a thing about champions, Iris. You don't know anything about them at all."

Iris closed her eyes and ignored Lemon. "I'm going to talk to Mrs. Chew," she said.

"Go ahead." Lemon squatted beside the sty and looked at Marvelous. "Don't worry about the fact that our pig is starving."

Mrs. Chew was still on her ladder. She pushed back her sun hat and stared at Iris crossing the grass.

"We have a new pig, Mrs. Chew!" Iris called.

"I've heard it barking."

"You couldn't have heard her, Mrs. Chew. She just got here," Iris called. "Anyway, pigs don't bark," she added.

Mrs. Chew climbed down the ladder. She hung up her paint bucket. She pushed her way through the honeysuckle hedge and walked over to the sty.

Marvelous came waddling up and peered at Mrs. Chew through the fence.

"She's a champion pig," Lemon said.

Mrs. Chew patted Marvelous. She left a spot of

red paint the size of a cherry between her eyes. "Looks healthy," she said.

"Except she won't eat," said Lemon. "She should be eating a lot and she won't. It worries me."

"I had an uncle like that," said Mrs. Chew.

"Who wouldn't eat?"

"Just Life Savers."

"Did he starve to death?" Iris asked.

"No. He ran in the Boston Marathon until he was seventy-two."

Lemon glanced at Iris. Iris was trying not to smile. "Well, that's really interesting, Mrs. Chew," Iris said. Iris always played along like that. Lemon didn't like to do it.

"Yes. I'd try Life Savers if I were you," Mrs. Chew repeated. "They worked for my uncle." She settled her sun hat so it shaded her eyes. "I've got to get back to my tree now," she said. "I want to finish up before hot weather."

Lemon and Iris watched Mrs. Chew climb back up her ladder. "Life Savers!" Iris giggled. "She's really crazy!"

Lemon made a face. "I'm going to see if Marvelous will eat a rose," she said.

Lemon picked a perfect Paul Scarlett from the trellis by the kitchen door. She laid it carefully on top of the food in the slops trough.

Marvelous wiggled her nose. She stood up and

looked into the trough. Then she bent down and nibbled a rose petal.

"She likes it!" Lemon said.

While Lemon and Iris watched, Marvelous ate the rose. She ate it daintily, petal by petal. She ate three carrot shavings. Then she lay down in the sun and crossed her hoofs.

"Well, now we know what champions like to eat," Iris said.

Lemon nodded. She looked nervously at the Soapstones' rosebushes. "I just hope they bloom a lot this summer," she said.

4

Lemon didn't see how a pig could grow fat on a diet of rose petals, but Marvelous began gaining weight. Mr. Soapstone weighed her every day. He recorded her weight on a piece of brown wrapping paper tacked to the kitchen wall.

At first he weighed her on Iris and Lemon's old baby scale. Then one day she wouldn't fit, so he carried her upstairs to weigh her on Mrs. Soapstone's own bathroom scale. After that Mrs. Soapstone ordered a hog scale and had it put in the garage.

Marvelous kept growing.

She was lovely and plump and white as lard. Her tail curled, and when she was in a good mood her grunt was gentle. Even Mrs. Soapstone had to admit that Marvelous was a beautiful pig.

"Beautiful!" Mr. Soapstone said. "Why, woman, that pig is spectacular! A sure-fire blue-ribbon champion or I'm a radish."

Lemon thought Marvelous was spectacular, too, but she worried about her disposition. Marvelous had moods. Some days she was as pleasant as a pig could be. Other days she was plain grouchy. There was no way of predicting what kind of day it would be ahead of time. On good days Marvelous grunted softly and ate rose petals from Lemon's hand. On bad days she lay on her back in a corner of the sty and ignored everyone. Lemon worried about her.

One night Lemon woke up very late. There were loud noises in the back yard. She'd been dreaming about Mrs. Chew walking on a tightrope, and at first the noises were mixed up with her dream.

Lemon rolled over and bumped into Iris. "Mutter snakes!" Iris growled. "Stem winders!"

Lemon sat up in bed. She *did* hear noises. In fact, what she heard was grunting. "Marvelous!" Lemon said out loud.

"Stir it!" said Iris.

Lemon jumped up and ran to the window. It was too dark to see the sty, but there was an awful commotion going on out there. Lemon put on her slippers and ran downstairs.

There was a light in the kitchen. The back door was open. Lemon peeped out into the darkness and listened. Marvelous had begun to grunt more softly. Then suddenly she stopped altogether. Maybe she was having a bad dream, Lemon thought. She yawned. "I may as well go back to bed," she said. And then Lemon heard another noise. She stopped in her tracks and stared out the door. It sounded to her like somebody singing.

Who would be singing? Lemon couldn't imagine. She tiptoed onto the back porch and peered at the sty. She definitely did hear somebody singing, and she could see a large pale blob at the corner of the fence. I've got to investigate, Lemon thought.

She tiptoed down the porch steps and across the wet grass. She crept along the honeysuckle bushes until she was near the sty. Then, at the same moment, she recognized the song and saw her father's striped pajamas. Mr. Soapstone was sitting on the slops trough singing "Martha."

"What are you *doing?*" Lemon whispered.

Mr. Soapstone jumped. He stopped singing. "Don't scare me," he said.

Mr. Soapstone was holding Marvelous in his arms. She had her snout in his pajama pocket. As soon as he stopped singing, she began to grunt softly. In a minute she was grunting out loud.

Mr. Soapstone began rocking her again. "She seems to be lonely," he said.

"I could hear her clear upstairs."

"She was making an awful racket," said Mr. Soapstone, "grunting and banging against the fence. I was afraid she'd bruise herself."

"I guess she wants out of her pen," said Lemon.

"As soon as I started rocking her, she calmed right down. You see, Lemon, these champions tend to be high strung."

"Are you going to rock her all night?" Lemon asked.

Marvelous grunted loudly. Mr. Soapstone rocked faster. "She seems to like me to sing," he said.

Lemon sat down on the trough beside her father. He sang "Martha" all over again. Marvelous sighed.

A light went on upstairs in Mrs. Chew's house. A window opened.

"Mrs. Chew'll call the police," Lemon said. "She's batty."

"Doubt she's ever raised a champion hog," said Mr. Soapstone. "She wouldn't understand their temperaments."

Marvelous squealed. Mr. Soapstone began singing again. All at once there was a crashing sound. A milk bottle hit the fence. Lemon looked up and saw Mrs. Chew disappearing.

"She's mad at us," Lemon whispered.

"Sorry for the racket, Mrs. Chew," Mr. Soapstone called.

Mrs. Chew slammed the window shut.

"Old fool," Mr. Soapstone muttered.

Marvelous began to squirm. She burrowed her head under Mr. Soapstone's arm. "You know," he

23

said, "I wouldn't be surprised if she were cold. A champion pig is delicate."

"I could take her to bed with me," Lemon said.

"I've been thinking of doing that myself," said Mr. Soapstone, "but I wonder whether your mother might get upset."

Lemon giggled.

"What about the oven?" said Mr. Soapstone. "That's an idea. We'll bundle her up in the oven."

"The oven?" Lemon said.

"Perfect place," said Mr. Soapstone.

They carried Marvelous into the kitchen. Mr. Soapstone opened the oven door and took out the metal racks. He made a nest of dish towels on the oven floor. "Snug and cozy," he said happily.

They tucked Marvelous into the oven. She stretched out full length, resting her head on the oven door. Mr. Soapstone took off his pajama top and rolled it up. He put it under her chin. Marvelous blinked drowsily.

"There now," said Mr. Soapstone. "You see, Lemon, a champion pig is a special kettle of fish."

Marvelous squirmed around, getting comfortable. She shut her eyes and sighed deeply.

"And we can't be too careful of her health," he added, padding toward the stairway.

"Won't she miss your singing?" Lemon asked.

Mr. Soapstone turned around. "I didn't think of that." They looked at Marvelous resting comfortably on Mr. Soapstone's pajama top. She was almost asleep.

"I'll turn on the radio," Mr. Soapstone said. "Just in case."

5

In the morning Lemon and Iris found their mother frying eggs on a hot plate on the back porch. She looked furious. "I don't know what the world is coming to," she said. "I think your father has gone out of his mind."

Lemon saw that Marvelous was still in the oven. She was not asleep. She was resting on her nest of towels. She blinked peacefully at Lemon.

"When your father proposed to me there was no mention made of raising pigs. If I had known that I would spend my middle age with a pig in my oven, I'd have thought twice."

Iris and Lemon decided to say nothing.

"We'll have to fumigate," said Mrs. Soapstone.

Mr. Soapstone came into the kitchen. He had bits of Kleenex stuck to his cheeks where he'd cut himself shaving. He walked over to the oven and scratched Marvelous. "Quite a peppy old girl," he said.

Mrs. Soapstone handed him a fried egg.

"Did you hear all that rumpus last night?" he asked.

"I heard nothing," said Mrs. Soapstone, "until, suddenly, this morning, while I was squeezing orange juice, I heard a grunt."

"I probably should have warned you," Mr. Soapstone said. He unfolded the newspaper.

"Is Marvelous going to live in the oven or what?" Iris asked.

"No. No. Only at night," Mr. Soapstone said.

"*Only* at night?" said Mrs. Soapstone.

Mr. Soapstone was reading the hog prices. "The hog market's holding strong," he said happily.

Lemon peeked at her mother. Mrs. Soapstone was looking at the ceiling.

Suddenly there was a clatter of bottles on the back porch. It was Mr. Hack delivering the milk. He stuck his head in the kitchen door to see if Mrs. Soapstone wanted any butter. "Say! There's a pig in your oven!" he said.

"It's our pig, Mr. Hack," said Iris. "She's a champion."

"No fooling?" said Mr. Hack. "That's a new one on me, keeping a pig in the oven."

"It's a new one on a lot of people," Mrs. Soapstone said grimly.

"I'll give you a good look at her," Mr. Soapstone

said. He lifted Marvelous onto the kitchen floor. "Pretty darn nice pig, wouldn't you say?"

Mr. Hack nodded.

"We're taking her to the County Fair," Iris said.

"For starters," Mr. Soapstone added. "With a pig like this no telling where you'll end up. Grand National? I wouldn't be surprised."

Mr. Hack clucked. "Well, that's a new one on me all right."

Marvelous sauntered over to Mr. Hack. She rubbed her head against his leg.

"She likes you!" Iris cried.

"Say, she's a pretty smart pig," said Mr. Hack. "More like a dog almost."

"Good blood," said Mr. Soapstone. "You can't beat good breeding."

Mr. Hack unloaded the milk bottles. He left a carton of cottage cheese for Marvelous.

"Do you think the blue-ribbon champion could go back to her sty now?" Mrs. Soapstone asked after Mr. Hack left.

Marvelous was eyeing the cottage cheese. She shook herself daintily and nosed the carton. Lemon emptied the cottage cheese into the slops bucket. She added a piece of buttered toast and a Fig Newton. "Come on, Marvelous," she said.

Lemon hoped that if she tried enough different kinds of food, she would find something Marvelous liked. Just to be on the safe side, she stopped to pick a rose. She saw Mrs. Chew standing on her back porch. Uh-oh, Lemon thought, she's still mad about last night.

Mrs. Chew was wearing a lavender sun hat. She stared straight at them. Lemon pretended not to see her. She let Marvelous into the sty and emptied the bucket into the slops trough. She watched for a moment to see what Marvelous would eat. Marvelous sniffed the trough, then picked up the rose and carried it to the opposite corner of the sty. Lemon sighed.

She picked up the pieces of broken milk bottle along the fence. She filled the water trough. Then she coiled up the hose, hooked the slops bucket over her arm, and started for the house.

"Wait a minute there!"

Mrs. Chew came climbing out between the honeysuckle bushes. She adjusted her sun hat. "I've come to call on your pig," she said.

"That's nice of you, Mrs. Chew," Lemon said. "I hope we didn't disturb you last night." She knew it was a dumb thing to say, but she wanted to be polite.

"Is your father going to sit in the pigpen and caterwaul like that every night?" Mrs. Chew asked.

"Oh, no."

"Just wondered. If so, I plan to sleep in my spare bedroom."

Marvelous was standing in the far corner of the sty, looking sideways at Mrs. Chew. "I brought that pig a praline," Mrs. Chew said.

"Thank you," said Lemon. "I'll give it to her for supper."

"I'll give it to her right now," said Mrs. Chew.

Marvelous turned her back to them and looked out through the fence. "She's a little shy," said Lemon.

"Didn't sound shy last night," said Mrs. Chew. "Come here, pig."

Marvelous edged along the fence with her eye on Mrs. Chew. Then she made a dash and scuttled under the slops trough. Lemon could see her peeking out from underneath.

"Come out of there, pig," said Mrs. Chew.

Marvelous was silent.

"Maybe if we kind of ignore her she'll come out," Lemon said.

"Not likely," said Mrs. Chew. "She reminds me of my sister."

Lemon began to worry. She wished that Mrs. Chew would go home. She could see Marvelous's eyes glittering under the slops trough. It made her nervous.

Mrs. Chew bent down and peered at Marvelous. "Can't see her." She picked up a rake and poked under the slops trough. "Sooey!" she said.

Marvelous grunted.

"Usually we don't poke her, since she's a champion and all," Lemon said.

"Champions come and go," said Mrs. Chew. She adjusted her sun hat. She opened the gate and walked into the sty.

Marvelous made a mean noise.

"I don't think you'd better do that, Mrs. Chew," Lemon said.

Mrs. Chew paid no attention. She walked over to

the slops trough. She got down on her hands and knees. She squinted underneath. "Out!" she said.

Marvelous wriggled farther under the trough.

Mrs. Chew reached under and grabbed Marvelous by the leg. "Out!" she repeated.

Then several things happened.

There was a sudden cloud of dust. The slops trough flew into the air and cottage cheese sprayed over the fence. Lemon thought a bomb had exploded.

There was a loud grunt. Somebody screeched. A streak of white flashed past Lemon's legs. A lavender sun hat whirled into the air. All around, it was raining cottage cheese and buttered toast. With a shattering crash the slops trough came down.

There was a ripping sound from the back porch. Mrs. Soapstone howled. Iris came flying out of the house, waving her arms. There was a terrible crash from farther away. Mrs. Soapstone yelled. "Out! Out! Get out!"

Iris looked at the sty and covered her mouth. From the house came a clatter of crockery. "Oh, oh, oh!" Iris gasped. There was another screech from the sty. Lemon and Iris closed their eyes.

All around them things clattered and banged. There were squawks from the sty. There were grunts from the house. Mrs. Soapstone kept shouting. Lemon and Iris held their breath. Then, all at once, there was silence.

Lemon peeked.

The dust was settling. Mrs. Chew sat on the slops trough adjusting her hat.

"What happened?" Iris whispered.

"Sssh," said Lemon.

Mrs. Soapstone came rushing out the door carrying Marvelous. "Take her," she yelled. "Get her out of here! All the breakfast dishes! Six plates! Two cups! The whole screen door! Who let her out?"

Lemon and Iris shook their heads. Lemon pointed at Mrs. Chew.

"It was her own decision," Mrs. Chew replied.

Mrs. Chew looked quite messy. Her dress was dotted with cottage cheese. A leaf of Bibb lettuce clung to her cheek.

"This is the end!" Mrs. Soapstone cried. "Enough is enough!" She wasn't even polite to Mrs. Chew. She turned her back and stalked off toward the house, muttering to herself and waving her arms.

Mrs. Chew stood up and straightened her dress. "Well," she said, "that was active." She popped the praline into her mouth and started toward the honeysuckle bushes. "My grandmother, you know, was a personal friend of Davy Crockett," she said as she disappeared.

"What did she say that for?" asked Iris.

"Because she's crazy," Lemon replied. "Why else would she do any of this?"

Lemon looked at the mess in the sty. She was mad. She knew terrible things were going to happen because of the dishes. "Why did you have to do it?" she said to Marvelous.

Marvelous tucked her snout under Lemon's collar and blinked peacefully.

"I'll help you clean up," Iris said.

"Oh, thank you, your highness," Lemon grumbled.

Marvelous lay down in the sun and grunted softly. Lemon and Iris cleaned the sty. That afternoon Mr. Soapstone sent Mrs. Soapstone two dozen yellow roses.

6

There were people Marvelous liked and there
were people she hated. Mr. Hack turned out to
be one of her favorites. He called on her three times
a week when he delivered the Soapstones' milk. As
soon as Marvelous heard bottles rattling, she began
to blink and grunt gently. She greeted Mr. Hack with
a happy snort. She looked at him sideways through
her eyelashes. Mr. Hack said Marvelous was the
smartest pig in the world. He always left her a carton
of cottage cheese.

Lemon and Iris pretended Marvelous loved cottage cheese in order not to hurt Mr. Hack's feelings.

"I think we ought to tell him," Iris said.

"No," said Lemon, "it would make him sad."

"I'm sick and tired of eating cottage cheese," said
Iris. "It makes me feel like throwing up."

Later Iris said, "Maybe we should ask Mr. Hack
to be Marvelous's godfather."

"What do you mean, 'godfather'?" Lemon asked.

"For her christening."

"You don't christen pigs, Iris."

"I have it all planned," Iris said.

Mr. Hack said he'd be pleased to be the godfather if they could have the christening some morning when he brought the milk.

"It has to be on a Wednesday," Iris said.

Mr. Hack said that would be all right.

Later Lemon got to wondering. "Why does it have to be a Wednesday?" she asked.

"Because that's the day Mother goes to her meeting," Iris said. "I was thinking she'd feel better if she didn't see Marvelous in the christening dress."

"You mean *our* christening dress?" said Lemon.

"I think it will be a perfect fit if we don't button it."

On Wednesday morning Iris was very busy. "I want it to be a really nice christening since Marvelous is a champion and all," she said.

She had a paper bag, which she tucked under the honeysuckle bushes. "That's the dress!" she whispered.

Lemon helped decorate the slops trough. They twined lilac leaves around it. "I want it to look like an altar," Iris said. She had a Mason jar of water she'd blessed, which she placed on the slops trough among the lilac leaves. She had borrowed their mother's prayer book.

"Really," said Iris, "we're all ready except for dressing Marvelous. And we can't do that till Mother leaves."

They sat in the shade of the crabapple tree waiting for Mrs. Soapstone to go to her meeting. They had to keep shooing Marvelous away from the altar. After a long time Mrs. Soapstone poked her head out the kitchen door and waved. "All right, let's go," said Iris.

Lemon held Marvelous. Iris tugged the christening dress over her head. Marvelous looked surprised.

"It's tight," Iris said. "I was afraid of that." She wiggled one front hoof through a sleeve.

Marvelous began squirming. "We should have done this before she started getting fat," Lemon panted.

Iris stuffed in Marvelous's other front hoof. Marvelous nibbled the lace around the sleeve. The dress gaped in back, but it looked very nice from the front, they thought.

"Just in time," Lemon said. "Here comes Mr. Hack." Mr. Hack had a bunch of daisies for Marvelous.

"I wasn't sure what to bring her," Mr. Hack said. "I wanted to bring something besides cottage cheese since it's a special occasion."

"Daisies are just perfect, Mr. Hack," Lemon said. "We needed flowers for the altar."

Mr. Hack looked happy. He carried the daisies

over to the slops trough and stuck them into the Mason jar.

"Not there!" Iris squawked.

Lemon punched her. "It's all right," she whispered. "We can use hose water."

"It's not blessed!" Iris hissed.

"Bless it as it runs out," said Lemon.

Marvelous was getting heavy. "Let's get started," Lemon said.

Iris went to get the hose. "I'm going to bless it right near the faucet," Iris said, "so when it comes out the end it'll already be holy."

"Mr. Hack, you have to hold Marvelous since you're the godfather," Lemon said.

Mr. Hack nodded. He looked very nice. He had on a black bow tie. He had stuck a daisy in the buttonhole of his milkman's jacket.

Marvelous snuggled up in Mr. Hack's arms and nibbled the daisy. Lemon straightened the christening dress as best she could.

"Stand by the altar, Mr. Hack," Iris said. She was holding the hose in one hand and the prayer book in the other. "I'm not going to read all this," she said, "just the main parts."

Lemon and Mr. Hack stood in front of Iris. Marvelous squirmed around to see what was going on. All at once Mrs. Chew's head poked out of the honeysuckle bushes. "I *thought* I heard milk bottles," she said.

7

Mr. Hack blushed. Marvelous growled. Mrs. Chew looked at Mr. Hack and Marvelous. She looked at Iris holding the hose. She walked over and lined up in front of the altar.

Lemon and Iris didn't know what to do.

"I *have* to start the ceremony," Iris said. "The holy water'll run out."

"Don't mind me," said Mrs. Chew.

Marvelous swiveled her head and glared at Mrs. Chew.

"Dearly beloved," Iris said nervously, "we are gathered here to christen our pig."

Marvelous gave a low, menacing grunt. "Never mind the prayers," Lemon said, "just do the water part."

Mr. Hack rocked Marvelous. He murmured to her, but Marvelous kept glaring at Mrs. Chew. Iris picked up the hose. "Okay," she said. "In the name of the Father, the Son, and the Holy Ghost, I christen this pig Marvelous—"

"Marvelous?" said Mrs. Chew. "All the pigs I know are called Penelope."

"Well, this one's called Marvelous," Iris said. "In the name of the Father—"

"Never mind all that," Lemon said nervously. "Just do it."

"I christen this pig Marvelous O'Hara Soapstone!"

Iris said triumphantly. Then she turned the hose full force on Marvelous's forehead.

Marvelous shot straight out of Mr. Hack's arms. She gave an ear-piercing squeal. Before anyone could stop her, Marvelous streaked through the honeysuckle bushes and out of sight. The last thing anyone saw was the lace hem of the christening dress disappearing into the bushes.

"Catch her!" Lemon screamed. She dived into the honeysuckle. Iris followed, still holding the hose. They pushed their way through the bushes into Mrs. Chew's yard.

"Watch the fresh paint!" Mrs. Chew shrieked.

They looked in all directions. There wasn't a trace of Marvelous anywhere. They ran around the house and looked down the street. Mr. Hack came puffing up behind them. "I should have held her tighter," he kept saying sadly.

They ran up and down the block looking under bushes. Mr. Hack looked under everyone's porch. He checked his truck. Lemon and Iris ran through every garage on the block. Marvelous simply was gone.

"I guess we'll have to call the police," Lemon said. "She could be anywhere by now."

"Maybe she'll come home by herself," Iris said. "Why don't we wait a little while."

Lemon was doubtful but she didn't know how to call the police. "I guess we could wait until lunch," she said.

Mr. Hack had to go on delivering milk. He kept apologizing. "I never expected her to jump. I should have had a better hold on her." Lemon and Iris tried to make him feel better, but they felt so awful themselves they couldn't do a very good job.

They walked home slowly. "What if she doesn't

come back?" Lemon said. "What if she crosses a street and a car hits her?"

"At least she's christened," Iris said.

"Oh, yes, that makes it all wonderful, doesn't it?" Lemon said. "If it hadn't been for the christening, she wouldn't be gone."

Iris didn't answer. Lemon glanced at her sister. "Where'd you get that O'Hara?" she asked. "We didn't talk about that."

"It just came to me while I was standing there," Iris said softly. She looked like she was going to cry.

Lemon put her arm around Iris's shoulders. "It's pretty," she said. "It's a good name. It goes just perfectly with Marvelous."

When they got home, the sty was still empty. Lemon had half-expected to see Marvelous waiting for them there. Mrs. Chew was gone. The lilac leaves on the altar were wilting. The hose still lay in the honeysuckle bushes, running water. "We may as well clean up the sty," Lemon said.

Iris turned off the hose. They wandered over to the sty and began picking up lilac leaves. They felt slow and sad. All they wanted was to hear a small grunt.

Lemon started raking the dirt. "Oh, look!" she said. She pointed to the slops trough.

Iris looked and started to cry. Mr. Hack had left a carton of cottage cheese standing next to the daisies.

8

Soon it was lunchtime. The noon whistle blew and faded away. Then it was after lunch. Mr. Pearl, the postman, delivered the mail. Mrs. Soapstone came home and went upstairs to clean the cedar closet. Marvelous did not return.

"We'll have to call Daddy," Lemon said.

"He'll tell Mother," said Iris.

"She'll find out anyway when she looks in the sty."

"Not about the dress!" Iris whispered.

Lemon had forgotten the dress. "Well, we'll have to call him anyway," she said.

"Gone! She can't be gone!" Mr. Soapstone yelled. "It's less than a month till the County Fair!"

"She is, though," Lemon said. "We can't find her anywhere."

"I'll be right home," said Mr. Soapstone.

Fifteen minutes later Mr. Soapstone came puffing into the house. He was bright red. His straw hat was tipped over one ear. "Call the police!" he shouted. "We'll organize a search party! Where's your mother?"

"She's cleaning the cedar closet," Iris said. "We'd better not disturb her."

"Nonsense!" Mr. Soapstone yelled. "This is an emergency!"

Mrs. Soapstone wasn't at all surprised. "Marvelous has always been disobedient," she said.

Mr. Soapstone telephoned the police. "I want to report a missing pig," he said. "Pure white." He shook his head. "No. No distinguishing marks."

Iris and Lemon glanced at each other. Mr. Soapstone frowned at the telephone. "Well, there can't be many lost pigs any one day," he said. "You'll recognize her right off. She is exceptionally intelligent."

Mrs. Soapstone looked at the ceiling. Lemon and Iris watched their father. Mr. Soapstone glared at the receiver. "No. Of course she isn't wearing a collar," he shouted. "No, nothing special! Isn't a runaway pig special enough?"

Lemon looked at Iris. "We have to tell him about the dress," she whispered.

Iris bit her lip.

"We *have* to," Lemon said.

Iris squirmed. She stood up and walked to the desk. "Daddy," she said. "There is one thing maybe that's special."

47

Mr. Soapstone spun around. "What!" he shouted. "Hold on there, Officer. What did you say?" he shouted at Iris.

"That maybe there's one special thing."

"Well, what is it? Speak up! This isn't a kindergarten picnic, you know!"

"She has on our christening dress," Iris muttered.

Mr. Soapstone stared at Iris. He stared at the wall. He shook his head. "Officer," he said, "the pig has on a christening dress."

He listened for a minute. Then he shouted, "What do you mean a description? How many pigs are you going to find running around in christening dresses?"

"It was trimmed with point d'esprit," said Mrs. Soapstone.

"I think I'll start looking for Marvelous right now," Iris said faintly.

"Hold on!" Mr. Soapstone slammed down the receiver. "Everyone will be assigned a territory. Nobody goes off till then."

Mrs. Soapstone wasn't saying a word. Mr. Soapstone got out the city map. He rummaged in his desk for a grease pencil. "Now," he said, spreading the map on the floor, "I will divide the town into fourths. Each of us will be responsible for searching thoroughly in his own fourth."

Mrs. Soapstone cleared her throat.

"Your mother will have all the territory between

the First Baptist Church and the river," Mr. Soapstone said, "bounded on the east by the City Hall and on the west by Mr. Pitkin's junk yard." Mr. Soapstone marked the area with his grease pencil. "You can start any time," he said.

Mrs. Soapstone frowned. She put on her glasses and looked at the map. Then she stood up. "The only reason I'm doing this," she said, "is because of the christening dress."

"I will take the center of town," said Mr. Soapstone, "because I don't believe it is appropriate for women and children to enter saloons. Iris will take this part nearest home because she's the youngest. Lemon will take this last piece which includes the park." Mr. Soapstone marked in the boundaries. "Now," he said, "let's go!"

Lemon and Iris studied their territories. Mrs. Soapstone closed the living-room windows in case of rain. Mr. Soapstone clapped on his straw hat. They set out in four separate directions from the front porch.

9

Lemon's territory started six blocks away, so she began to run. "Still looking for your pig?" Mrs. Chew called as Lemon shot past her house. Mrs. Chew was on the roof painting a vine on her chimney.

"Yes, I am," Lemon shouted.

"Could be she's left town," Mrs. Chew yelled after her.

Lemon was sick and tired of Mrs. Chew. Personally she thought that if Mrs. Chew hadn't come to the christening Marvelous might not have run away. She was glad when she was out of sight.

Lemon hurried along to the corner of Pine Street where her territory began. She stopped to catch her breath. There was a church on the corner. The door was open. Lemon guessed she'd better check inside.

There was a crowd of people outside the church. Lemon couldn't decide whether they were going in or coming out. She hoped they wouldn't notice her. She ran up the church steps two at a time. In the vestibule were several ladies in bridesmaids' dresses. "Uh-oh, a wedding," Lemon muttered. She tiptoed around behind them. Maybe I can get a look before the wedding starts, she thought.

A few people were already sitting down. Lemon squatted and peeked under the first row of pews. She doubted that Marvelous was in the church. But I have to check thoroughly, she thought.

She crept backward slowly along the side aisle, checking each row of pews as she passed it. She was concentrating so hard she almost ran into a man who was standing in the aisle. She straightened up fast and pushed back her hair. "Excuse me," she said. "I was looking for my pig."

"I beg your pardon?" said the man. He was the minister, Lemon realized. He was small and plump and didn't look happy.

"We've lost our pig," Lemon explained. "I thought she might have come in here."

"This is a church," the minister said.

"Yes, I know," said Lemon, "but the door was open."

"We're about to have a wedding," the minister said. "Perhaps you can look for your pig another time."

"It's kind of an emergency," Lemon said. "Otherwise I wouldn't bother you."

The minister cleared his throat. "Does your pig have a name?" he asked. "Perhaps we could call her softly."

"Her name's Marvelous," said Lemon. "I *could* call her, but I'm not sure she'd come. Pigs are different from dogs, you know. The best thing is just to check under all the pews myself."

The minister coughed. The organ started to play softly. Lemon noticed that people were beginning to fill the pews. "I'll hurry," she said.

"Wait!" the minister whispered. "You can't do it now. The bridal party will be coming in."

Lemon felt awful. She must have looked awful. "Give me a description," the minister said. "If I see a pig I'll hold it for you."

Lemon grinned. "That's awfully nice of you," she said. "Her name is Marvelous, like I said. She's white with a pink snout and grayish-black hoofs. More black, I guess, than gray. And—"

"I'll recognize her," said the minister.

Lemon smiled. "Thank you," she said. "That's wonderful. Oh, one more thing," Lemon whispered. "She's wearing a christening dress."

The minister gave her an odd look. Lemon started for the door. She hurried down the church steps. That had taken quite a while, and she had only just begun searching her territory.

The next block was lined on either side with

flower gardens. Every house had flowers in bloom, and almost every flower was a rose. Lemon felt hopeful. If Marvelous found this street, she'd never leave, Lemon thought.

She began searching systematically. She tried to look into every rose bed and behind every trellis. Besides ordinary rosebushes there were climbing roses and rose arbors and tangled hedges of wild pink roses. There really were too many. Lemon began to hate the smell of them. Worst of all she could find no trace of Marvelous, not even a nibbled petal.

Maybe somebody else has found her, Lemon thought. What if I spend all day climbing through people's rose beds and garages and all the while Marvelous has been found? She felt like going home. She knew she hadn't better.

At the next corner Lemon was surprised to see Iris leaning against a Stop sign. "I was looking for you," Iris said. "I finished my territory."

"How could you have?" said Lemon. "I've only finished my second block."

"I just rang everyone's doorbell and asked if they'd seen a pig," Iris said. "Nobody had."

"I'm afraid something bad has happened. I have an awful feeling."

"I was thinking we should buy some ice cream and sit in the shade and try to think where we'd go if we were Marvelous."

"I can't even guess where Marvelous would go," Lemon said.

"That's why I was thinking of getting ice cream," Iris replied. "In my experience it helps you to figure things out."

10

They found an ice cream truck at the edge of the park. Lemon bought a Popsicle. Iris had an Eskimo Pie. They sat down on a bench and licked for a while. "This isn't helping my thinking at all," said Lemon.

"Give it time," said Iris.

Lemon started the second half of her Popsicle. She was tired. She leaned back and stared at a fat cloud overhead. Iris yawned.

Suddenly Lemon sat bolt upright.

"Did you hear something funny?" she said.

"Nope."

"Listen."

"All I hear is the stuff I always hear."

"No. Listen. I thought I heard a grunt." They listened hard. There it was again! This time there was no doubt about it. It was definitely a grunt.

"I heard it!" Iris shouted.

Lemon jumped up. "It came from over by the fountain!"

They flew down the gravel path toward the fountain, dodging cats and dogs and children on bikes. "I know that grunt came from this direction," Lemon cried. "Marvelous must be around here somewhere."

They raced around a clump of bushes. Suddenly Iris cried, "There she is!"

The park fountain was surrounded by a lily pond. Marvelous was standing in plain sight among the lilies. The christening dress floated out behind her.

In the center of the pond was a large cement dolphin. Water spouted from its mouth into the pond. Marvelous grunted at him.

"Marvelous! Marvelous! Here we are!" Iris shouted. "You're saved!"

Marvelous turned and looked calmly at Lemon and Iris.

"Don't worry, Marvelous, you're safe now!" Iris called.

Marvelous didn't seem to be worrying. She blinked at Iris, then turned back to the dolphin. She grunted softly and rubbed her snout against his side.

"What's she doing?" Iris said.

Marvelous walked slowly around the dolphin, trailing the christening dress. She looked at him sideways through her eyelashes. Her ears twitched.

"Come here, Marvelous," Lemon called.

Marvelous didn't pay the slightest attention. She lay her head on the dolphin and grunted quietly.

"Maybe she's sick," Iris said. "Maybe her head aches."

"She acts sort of sick," Lemon agreed.

"Marvelous, honey," Iris called, "come over here a minute."

Marvelous seemed not to have heard a word. She rubbed her head against the dolphin's side.

"She's acting just like she does with Mr. Hack!" Lemon exclaimed.

"Maybe she thinks that *is* Mr. Hack!" Iris said. "Maybe she's gone blind."

"Don't be stupid."

"Well, something's funny."

"Come here, Marvelous," Lemon said firmly. "Time to go home."

Marvelous looked at Lemon. Then she walked around to the other side of the dolphin.

"She doesn't want to come home!" said Iris.

"She has to."

"You know what I think?" Iris said. "I think she's fallen in love with the dolphin."

"It's a fountain!" said Lemon.

"That's what I think, though. She's acting exactly like that stupid Mavis Pine did before she got married."

Lemon walked around the pool and studied Marvelous. She *was* acting something like Mavis Pine. "Well, I can't help it if she's in love," Lemon said. "She's got to come home. If she won't come out, we'll have to go in after her."

Lemon sat down and took off her sneakers. "You've got to help," she said.

Together they waded into the lily pond. The bottom was slimy. Marvelous stood still and watched them coming. "Time to go home," Iris kept saying, but Marvelous didn't budge. She grunted a low, nasty grunt and shook herself. She splattered water all over Lemon.

Lemon was beginning to get mad. "This is your last chance, Marvelous," she said. Marvelous turned her head away.

"All right," Lemon said. "You asked for it." She made a dive for Marvelous's neck. Suddenly she skidded and plopped into the water. She came up spitting. She was furious.

"You push from behind and I'll pull her," Lemon sputtered. "Darn pig!" She grabbed Marvelous around the neck. Iris shoved. Marvelous began to jump and kick. "Push!" Lemon yelled.

"I *am* pushing," Iris shouted. "She won't move."

Lemon held tight to Marvelous's neck. She yanked. Marvelous moved a step. Iris slipped. Her head disappeared under the lily pads. Marvelous jumped backward. She ran around the dolphin and stood on the other side, grunting loudly. Iris popped up between the lilies. "I'm going to get Daddy!" she yelled.

Marvelous glared at them as they crawled out of the pond. "That's the worst pig I've ever known," said Iris. Long, slimy lily stems were hanging from her hair, and Iris hated anything slimy. "She should be ashamed of herself."

Marvelous was leaning on the dolphin's side. Now and then she snorted. Lemon could see she didn't care at all.

They sloshed home as fast as they could. Greenish water ran down their backs, leaving a trail on the sidewalk. "I could easily catch pneumonia from this," said Iris.

11

Mr. Soapstone was standing on the front porch looking down the street through binoculars. "We found her!" Lemon yelled. Mr. Soapstone lowered the binoculars and made a *V* for victory.

"Where is she?"

Lemon and Iris sloshed up the porch steps. "She's in the lily pond in the park," Lemon said. "We can't make her come home."

"Did you try calling to her?" Mr. Soapstone asked.

Iris snorted.

"The thing is," Lemon said, "I think Marvelous is in love."

"Nonsense," said Mr. Soapstone. "She's too young to be in love."

"I think she is, though. I think she's in love with that cement dolphin in the middle of the lily pond."

"Hogwash," Mr. Soapstone said. "That's a ridiculous idea. Marvelous is much too intelligent for that."

Iris and Lemon stood on the porch dripping. Mr. Soapstone clapped on his straw hat. "A cement dolphin, indeed!" he said. "I'll go have a talk with her."

Marvelous saw them coming. She turned away and looked at the dolphin. "You see?" Lemon said.

Mr. Soapstone stalked to the side of the lily pond. "Marvelous! I want your attention!" he called. "It's time to go home."

Marvelous didn't even blink.

"I said it's time to go home!" Mr. Soapstone shouted.

Marvelous didn't move.

"These champions!" Mr. Soapstone shook his head. "They take special handling." He squatted down and clucked gently. "Come on out of there, old girl."

Marvelous turned her head to look at Mr. Soapstone. She blinked. Then she turned away again.

"Marvelous," Mr. Soapstone said, "this foolishness has gone on long enough. You come on out of there or I'll come in and get you."

Marvelous continued to ignore him. Lemon began feeling sorry for her father.

"I command you to come here!" Mr. Soapstone called.

Nothing happened.

"Immediately!" Mr. Soapstone shouted.

62

Nothing.

Mr. Soapstone sat down on the pond ledge. "Be reasonable, Marvelous," he said. "That thing isn't even alive. It's a Municipal Park Authority cement fountain!"

Marvelous blinked at the dolphin. She purred.

"You're being ridiculous!" Mr. Soapstone shouted.

Suddenly Lemon got the giggles. It was a silly thing to do, but she couldn't help it. Mr. Soapstone glared at her. "I don't see what's so funny about a grand champion hog behaving like an idiot," he said.

He turned back to the pond. "Marvelous!" he shouted. "I'm coming in after you."

Marvelous did nothing. She watched Mr. Soapstone take off his shoes and his socks. He rolled up his trouser legs. Then he tested the water with his toe. Mr. Soapstone hated cold water.

"Marvelous, I'll give you one more chance!" Mr. Soapstone shouted. "I'll count to three." He counted to three. Marvelous didn't move.

Mr. Soapstone scowled at Lemon and Iris. He settled his straw hat firmly on his head. He stepped into the lily pond.

Marvelous grunted. Mr. Soapstone waded toward her. Marvelous watched him. When Mr. Soapstone got within arm's reach, Marvelous ran around to the other side of the dolphin. "Halt!" yelled Mr. Soapstone.

Lemon and Iris hung over the edge of the lily

pond. Mr. Soapstone crept stealthily around the front of the dolphin. Marvelous squealed and shot off around the tail. Mr. Soapstone followed.

Around they went, first Marvelous, then Mr. Soapstone. Marvelous squealed. Mr. Soapstone swore. Water sloshed over the edge of the pond. The lilies bounced on the surface. A lady with a baby carriage stopped to watch. Mr. Soapstone shouted. He plunged around the dolphin in water up to his knees.

Mr. Soapstone was gaining on Marvelous. She ran as fast as she could, but Mr. Soapstone's legs were longer. He lunged for her and caught a hoof. Marvelous howled. She flailed. Great waves of water washed over the pond edge. "Got you now!" Mr. Soapstone shouted triumphantly. He grabbed Marvelous around the middle. His hat went spinning into the lily pond. Marvelous kicked. It was no use. Mr. Soapstone held her firmly and waded out of the pond.

"Carry my shoes," he growled to Iris. Lemon fished out his hat as it floated past. The lady with the baby carriage pushed off toward the playground. Together Mr. Soapstone and Lemon and Iris started for home. Marvelous howled pitifully. She was furious. She wouldn't look at any of them. The christening dress trailed over Mr. Soapstone's arm and dripped water on the sidewalk. The dress was green with algae.

After a few blocks Mr. Soapstone stopped to get a better hold on Marvelous. Lemon peeped up at his face. To her surprise, he was smiling. "Quite an old girl," he said happily. "Plenty spunky, wouldn't you say?"

Marvelous closed her eyes and howled.

12

Mrs. Soapstone threw the christening dress into the rubbish can. Mr. Soapstone hosed off Marvelous and put her in the sty. Lemon and Iris were sent to their room. Marvelous crawled under the slops trough and closed her eyes.

Marvelous wouldn't eat supper. In the morning she wouldn't eat breakfast. She lay under the slops trough and kept her eyes closed.

Mr. Hack drove up at nine o'clock with a carton of raspberry yoghurt. He got down on his knees and clucked to Marvelous. She sighed and buried her snout in the dust.

At ten thirty Mrs. Chew came to call. "I made that pig a floating island custard," she said. Marvelous didn't even bother to growl.

All day Marvelous lay under the slops trough with her eyes shut. Lemon sat beside the fence and worried. Iris brought out her recorder and played "Sweet

Betsy from Pike." Marvelous lay like a dead pig under the slops trough.

"I think we ought to call the veterinarian," Mrs. Soapstone said at suppertime. "I don't want her to die in the back yard."

"I think she misses the dolphin," said Lemon.

"Ridiculous," said Mr. Soapstone. "Champion pigs don't fall in love with fountains."

The next morning Mr. Soapstone dragged Marvelous out from under the slops trough. She didn't wiggle or kick. She just let herself be dragged. He carried her to the hog scale and laid her on it. "She's lost three pounds!" he exclaimed to Lemon. He felt her nose. He listened to her heart. Marvelous opened her eyes slowly and gave Lemon a forlorn look. Then she closed them.

"At this rate she won't make the hog judging!" Mr. Soapstone said. "She won't be fat enough to enter."

Lemon knew how much it meant to her father to win first prize in the hog category. "Maybe we'd better buy the dolphin for her," she said.

Mr. Soapstone snorted. "There are more ways than one to skin a cat," he said.

Lemon didn't know what her father meant, but she knew he must have a plan in mind. It made her feel a lot better all morning, knowing her father had thought of something.

Iris got out her recorder again. "Would Marvelous like 'Bluebells of Scotland,' or would it make her sad, do you think?"

"Try it," said Lemon.

Iris played "Bluebells of Scotland" all the way through twice without a mistake. She was starting for the third time when Marvelous sighed so deeply it scared them.

"It's no use," Lemon said.

"It's my most cheerful piece," said Iris.

Nobody felt like lunch. Even Mrs. Soapstone was upset. "I *don't* know why your father won't call a doctor," she said. She was getting ready to call one herself when they heard Mr. Soapstone come in the back door.

"I think I've solved our problem," Mr. Soapstone said.

"I certainly hope so," said his wife.

Mr. Soapstone went back to the car. He lifted a fat spotted pig out of the trunk.

"Not *another* pig!" said Mrs. Soapstone.

"A companion for Marvelous," Mr. Soapstone said. "I don't entirely approve myself. Marvelous strikes me as too young for this sort of thing, but we have to remember the Fair is coming. She's got to eat."

"*Two* pigs!" said Mrs. Soapstone.

"Better than a cement fish."

Mr. Soapstone carried the new pig to the sty. He

unlatched the gate and pushed the pig inside. Lemon thought the new pig looked nice enough. She hoped Marvelous would think so.

"Is that a male pig, you mean?" Iris asked.

"Certainly," said Mr. Soapstone.

"And you hope Marvelous will fall in love with him instead?"

"Well, of course she will," Mr. Soapstone replied. "Marvelous is an intelligent pig."

Mr. Soapstone latched the gate and climbed up on the fence. Lemon and Iris clambered up beside him. They sat in a row and waited to see what would happen.

The new pig trotted along the fence, sniffing the ground. Marvelous lay under the slops trough with her eyes closed. The new pig rooted in the dust along the fence, grunting. Marvelous didn't seem to know he was there.

All at once the new pig spied the slops trough. He trotted over and nosed the food that had accumulated since Marvelous stopped eating. Lemon saw the hair on Marvelous's neck bristle.

The pig thrust his nose into the slops and snorted. He stuck his whole head into the trough and began to eat. Lemon and Iris had never seen a pig eat like that before.

"Will you look at that appetite!" Mr. Soapstone said happily.

There was a low grumble from under the slops

trough. The new pig didn't seem to hear it. He snorted and dug his snout deeper. Personally Lemon thought the way the new pig ate was repulsive. She was used to Marvelous.

The pig blew a bubble in the slops.

"That's a champion's appetite!" Mr. Soapstone said.

"Ick!" said Lemon.

The new pig licked up the last bit of hog mash. He snorted with satisfaction. Hog mash dripped from his snout. Carrot shavings clung to his ears. He lay down and rolled in the dust, scratching his back and grunting.

Lemon thought he was perfectly disgusting. She saw two eyes glittering under the slops trough. She wondered what Marvelous was thinking.

All at once the new pig stopped rolling and sat up. His ears twitched. He snuffed at the dust around the trough, then grunted loudly. "He sees Marvelous!" Iris whispered.

"Aha!" said Mr. Soapstone.

The new pig snorted. He pawed the dirt with his front roof. Marvelous made a low rumbling noise deep in her throat.

"What's the matter with Marvelous?" Iris said.

"She's falling in love," said Mr. Soapstone. "That's a pig's courting call."

It didn't sound that way to Lemon.

The new pig walked around the trough and peered

under from the other side. Marvelous rumbled again, louder. The new pig stuck his head clear under the slops trough. Marvelous made an awful noise. The slops trough began to rock. Marvelous snarled. Her head shot out from underneath.

The new pig backed up.

Marvelous crawled out and walked forward slowly, making low, angry noises. The new pig backed into the fence. He glanced around and saw he could go no farther. Marvelous kept walking toward him. The pig grunted nervously. Marvelous snarled.

The pig began walking sideways along the fence, keeping his eye on Marvelous. Then suddenly he broke into a run. Marvelous shot after him. She chased him round and round the fence. Whirlwinds of dust rose in the air.

"I don't think they're in love at all!" Iris screamed. "I think she's going to kill him!"

Mr. Soapstone jumped into the sty. Every time a pig shot by, Mr. Soapstone tried to grab it. It was hard to see the pigs through the dust. First a spotted streak rocketed past, then a white one. Spotted, then white. White. Spotted. The pigs squealed. Mr. Soapstone shouted. Lemon and Iris held on to each other.

Bits of foam mixed with the dust. The pigs gasped as they dashed by. "They're wearing out!" Mr. Soapstone cried.

The new pig staggered around once more. His

eyes were glassy. His sides foamed. He loped to the gate of the sty and collapsed, gasping.

Marvelous stopped, panting hard. She surveyed the new pig lying in the dust. Then she walked over and bit him.

"Get him out of there!" Iris screamed. "Marvelous is going to eat him up!"

Mr. Soapstone bent over the new pig. "She just nicked him," he said.

"But if we leave them alone, she'll kill him!" said Iris.

Mr. Soapstone climbed over the fence. "Don't be silly," he said. "You don't understand pigs. They take a while getting used to each other. In a day or two it will all be different."

13

Marvelous didn't get used to the new pig. He sat in a corner of the sty for two days, watching her. Marvelous wouldn't let him near the slops trough. If he grunted, she snarled. If he tried to move, she bit him.

"This can't go on!" Mrs. Soapstone said. "You're going to have to do something about it."

On the third day Mr. Soapstone gave up. He loaded the new pig into the car and took him away. "We never even named him!" Iris said. But Lemon was relieved to see him go.

"He wasn't the kind of pig Marvelous would like," she said.

Marvelous watched until the car disappeared. Then she crawled back under the trough and closed her eyes.

"What are we going to do?" said Lemon. "She's going to die of a broken heart unless we do something."

"Maybe we should kind of leave the gate open," Iris said.

"And let her escape again?"

"Well, if she wants to."

"We can't," Lemon said. "We just can't."

Marvelous did not improve. Her ears drooped. Her hair was matted. She hardly ever opened her eyes. By the end of the week, when Mr. Soapstone weighed her, she had lost another four pounds. Mr. Soapstone looked at Marvelous lying on the scales. Her ribs were beginning to show. "Oh, all right!" he said to her. "Have it your way."

Late that afternoon a truck pulled into the Soapstones' driveway. Lemon was sitting in the sty feeding Marvelous sugar water with an eyedropper. A man in blue overalls got out of the truck. "Is this the place that's got the sick pig?" he asked.

"Yes," Lemon answered, "but I know she'll get better." Lemon was afraid he was going to take Marvelous away.

"Well, I got a present for her," the man said.

He turned his truck around slowly. Lemon could see there was something big covered with canvas in the back. "He's bringing you a present, Marvelous!" Lemon said. The pig paid no attention.

The truck backed slowly down the driveway. Then it turned and began backing across the lawn. "You're on the grass!" Lemon cried.

The truck backed over the rose bed.

The man in overalls craned his head out of the cab. "How'm I doing?" he yelled. Lemon didn't know what to say. She could see a floribunda rosebush resting on the truck's back fender.

"I think you're close enough," she called.

The man came around to the back of the truck. "This thing I got's supposed to go inside that fence," he said.

"What is it?" Lemon asked.

"You got me," said the man. "I just picked it up this way."

He climbed into the rear of the truck and shoved. He pushed and pulled the big canvas bundle to the edge. Then he slid it down a board to the gate in the fence. "This thing must weigh more than the Statue of Liberty," he said.

The canvas was bound tight with ropes. Lemon grabbed some rope and helped the man tug. Marvelous crawled out from under the slops trough and watched suspiciously.

They pushed and tugged the canvas-covered object to the center of the sty. "How's this?" the man said. "Looks like as good a spot as any."

"Yes, that's fine," Lemon said. She could hardly wait to see what was under the canvas.

"Well, okay then." The man in overalls took out his pocketknife. He cut the rope in several places

and unwound it. Lemon helped him pull off the canvas.

Marvelous squealed. There, in the center of the sty, stood the dolphin!

"Will you look at that pig!" the man exclaimed.

Marvelous was prancing around the dolphin as though she'd gone crazy. She jumped into the air and grunted. She pawed the ground and squealed.

"Looks like she's got a screw loose!" the man said.

"She's just happy," Lemon replied. "She's very emotional for a pig."

Marvelous was raising such a rumpus that Mrs. Chew looked out her window. Mrs. Soapstone and Iris came running out the back door.

"What in the world?" cried Mrs. Soapstone. "Your father must have lost his mind!"

"Looks like that pig's plugged into a socket," called Mrs. Chew.

Iris and Lemon smiled at each other. The man in overalls folded up the canvas. "That sure must be some crazy kind of pig," he said. "I never heard of buying a statue for a pig before."

"She's a champion pig," Lemon said with dignity.

"Yeah? Well she sure must be *something* special."

Marvelous kept jumping up and down. She made so much noise it was impossible to hear anyone talk. Mrs. Chew came climbing through the bushes. She and Mrs. Soapstone and the man in overalls leaned on the fence and shook their heads. Then one by one they left until only Lemon and Iris were sitting beside the sty.

Marvelous kept circling the dolphin, admiring him from every angle. She rubbed him with her snout. Occasionally she gave a satisfied grunt. At last she curled up beside him, and after a few minutes she fell asleep.

The sun was low. Mrs. Chew was on her back porch shelling peas. Lemon and Iris squatted beside the sty playing jacks on an orange crate. They could smell their dinner cooking. The sun turned the dolphin a lovely cantaloupe color. Marvelous dozed peacefully beside him. Everything seemed right again.

Mr. Soapstone's car turned into the driveway. Lemon and Iris waved. Mr. Soapstone looked at the ruts in the lawn. He looked at the ruts in his rose bed. Then he took a good long look at the cantaloupe-colored dolphin.

"Look how *happy* Marvelous is," said Lemon.

"That was just a wonderful thing for you to do," said Iris.

Mr. Soapstone sighed. He pushed back his straw hat and headed for the house. He looked tired.

"You know it's nice to have Marvelous feeling well again," Mrs. Soapstone said at supper. "It bothered me when she was so listless."

Mr. Soapstone stirred his iced tea. He was the only person still looking grumpy.

"Well, I hope she's satisfied," he said.

14

Marvelous began behaving in a way most un-usual for her. First Lemon noticed how much she ate. She ate everything in her trough each time it was filled. Her manners improved. When Mrs. Chew came to call, she no longer hid under the slops trough. When Mr. Hack brought her cottage cheese, she ate it. Lemon and Iris felt perfectly safe when they forgot to close the sty gate. Marvelous never strayed far from the dolphin.

"She's getting to be a very nice pig," said Mrs. Soapstone.

Marvelous was gaining weight again. Her sides filled out. Her ribs disappeared. Mr. Soapstone weighed her every day as usual. He had to keep the hog scale in the sty because Marvelous wouldn't leave the dolphin.

"Will Marvelous be fat enough for the Fair?" Lemon asked one day.

"Looks that way," said Mr. Soapstone.

"I suppose you've arranged to take the dolphin along?" asked Mrs. Soapstone.

"I have *not,*" Mr. Soapstone replied. "Don't talk nonsense. Surely they can stand to be parted for a day."

"You may be surprised," said Mrs. Soapstone.

The night before the Fair, Lemon and Iris fed Marvelous early. They wanted her to have a good night's sleep. Mr. Soapstone had borrowed a trailer for Marvelous to ride in to the Fair. He was padding it with burlap bags. Marvelous finished her supper and curled up by the dolphin. Mrs. Soapstone came out and leaned on the fence.

"She really does look like a champion," Mrs. Soapstone said. "Your father's been right all along."

"I'm worried about tomorrow though," said Lemon. "Marvelous won't like leaving the dolphin behind."

Mr. Soapstone finished padding the trailer. "I want Marvelous to try it out," he said. "We'll go for a short ride."

He opened the sty gate. "Come on, old girl," he said.

Marvelous blinked peacefully.

Mr. Soapstone whistled. Marvelous didn't move. Mr. Soapstone picked her up and carried her to the trailer. "Sometimes I forget she isn't a dog," he said.

Marvelous wasn't happy about the trailer. She kept peering over the side and grunting nervously.

"You ought to make arrangements for the dolphin," Mrs. Soapstone said again.

"I don't want to hear any more of that foolishness," said Mr. Soapstone. He started the car and looked behind him. He backed slowly out the driveway. Lemon and Iris stood on the curb watching Marvelous. They could see her snout peeping anxiously over the trailer side.

"Back in a minute!" Mr. Soapstone called. "We'll just go around the block."

Lemon and Iris turned back to the sty. "She needs fresh water," Lemon said. "Get the hose." Iris dragged the hose across the lawn. Lemon dumped the stale water. Just as they were refilling the water trough, Marvelous strolled in the gate.

"That was quick," Lemon said. "It seems as though they just left."

"How did she like the trailer?" Iris called. Then she stopped. Mr. Soapstone and the trailer were not in sight.

Marvelous was out of breath.

"Where's Daddy?" Iris said.

"Oh, boy!" said Lemon. "She must have jumped out."

Just then Mr. Soapstone pulled into the driveway. He looked pleased. "That trailer's going to work just fine," he said. "Marvelous loved it. Not a peep out of her the whole ride."

"But—" Lemon said.

"A pig likes motion," Mr. Soapstone explained. "It makes her drowsy."

"But Marvelous—" Iris exclaimed.

"Now let's tuck her in for a good night's sleep." Mr. Soapstone walked over to the trailer and looked in. From the sty came a grunt. Mr. Soapstone turned around. He had a funny expression on his face.

"I was trying to tell you that Marvelous came back early," Lemon said.

Mr. Soapstone did not reply. His lips got very thin. He went straight to the cellar. Later he came up with a roll of clothesline and some heavy rope. He put them in the trailer. He glared at the dolphin. He scowled at Marvelous. Then he went to bed without saying a word to anyone.

15

The next morning Lemon and Iris were up almost as soon as the sun. They hurried to the sty with Marvelous's breakfast. While they waited for her to finish, Lemon collected a scrub brush and a bottle of bath salts. Iris filled a pail with warm water at the kitchen sink.

They bathed Marvelous thoroughly, taking special trouble with her ears. They rubbed her dry and brushed her smooth. They polished her hoofs until they shone. Finally they tied a pleated, sky-blue ruff around her neck. She looked spectacular. The bath salts gave her a faint odor of June geranium.

Marvelous looked at her hoofs. She twisted around and looked at the ruff. She gazed sideways at Lemon through her eyelashes.

"She knows she's beautiful," Iris said.

"Now if only she won't roll in the dust until we're ready to go," said Lemon.

Marvelous seemed to know she shouldn't roll in

the dust. She walked all the way around the sty, taking tiny steps. Lemon and Iris had never seen her walk that way before. Every so often she stopped and peeped over her ruff at the dolphin.

"Why's she acting so funny?" Iris said. "Do you think that's what champions are supposed to act like?"

Mrs. Chew came stumbling out of the honeysuckle bushes. "I've made something for that pig," she said. She had a huge roll of paper in her arms. "It's to go on the back of the trailer," she explained. She unrolled her paper and thumbtacked it to the trailer. Then she stood back and narrowed her eyes. She got out a paintbrush and dabbed at the paper. "There," she said.

Lemon and Iris looked at the paper. It was a large hand-painted sign. It said, BON VOYAGE, PIG.

"That's very nice," said Lemon. It was nice. The letters were in red, white, and blue, alternating. The O's, one G, and the I didn't show up very well because they were white.

"That's beautiful!" Iris said.

"I think so," said Mrs. Chew.

Mr. Soapstone thought the sign was silly. "This is a business trip," he said.

He backed the trailer down the driveway. "All in for the fair," he shouted. Mrs. Soapstone and Iris got into the car.

Mr. Soapstone uncoiled the clothesline. "This time Marvelous is going to be tied in," he said. "No more funny business."

That made Lemon feel terrible. She knew how Marvelous would hate being tied. "I'll sit with her in the trailer," she said.

"Nonsense!" said Mr. Soapstone.

He lifted Marvelous into the trailer. He tied the clothesline around her middle and then bound the ends tight to the trailer. He was very gentle, but Marvelous squealed. She was furious. She lowered her head and grunted angrily. She squirmed, but the clothesline held her fast.

Lemon tried feeding her a rose petal. "It's going to be all right," she whispered. Marvelous closed her eyes.

"Hop in now," Mr. Soapstone said. Lemon got into the car reluctantly. Marvelous was straining to see the dolphin. Lemon felt awful.

"I wish you'd let me sit with her," she said.

"It's against the law to ride back there," said Mr. Soapstone. "You watch, Marvelous will be fine as soon as we're on our way."

He started the engine. Marvelous howled. They bounced out into the street with Marvelous making a terrible racket. Mrs. Chew was standing on her front porch, waving. Mr. Hack pulled his milk truck over to the curb to let them by. "Good luck!" he called as they bumped past him. Mr. Soapstone gave him the victory sign.

Marvelous let out an awful howl. Mr. Soapstone speeded up. They rounded the corner, bumping and rattling. People stopped to watch as they sped by with Marvelous howling and Mrs. Chew's sign flapping in the breeze.

16

When they got out into the country, Marvelous quieted down. "You see?" said Mr. Soapstone. "Pigs have short memories."

Lemon looked at Marvelous standing in the trailer, jouncing slightly from side to side. Her sky-blue ruff was askew. Her ears drooped. Now and then she howled.

"She looks broken-hearted to me," Iris said.

Lemon nodded. Marvelous was beginning to look awful again.

"Wait till she sees the Fair," Mr. Soapstone said. "She'll perk right up. She hasn't got champion's blood for nothing."

After a few more miles the traffic got heavy. The Soapstones joined a line of cars headed into the fairgrounds. Cars bounced past them on either side. People craned to read Mrs. Chew's sign. They whistled and waved at Marvelous. "They know something special when they see it!" Mr. Soapstone said happily. But Lemon was worried.

They saw the Ferris wheel before anything else. It was already turning high in the sky. On every side there were striped awnings and bright canvas tents. Whole families carrying picnic baskets and raincoats piled out of cars. Mr. Soapstone stopped to ask the way to the Hog Pavilion.

The Hog Pavilion was at the far end near the midway. Each hog was assigned a stall. The stalls were nice, Lemon thought. They were small, but each one was spread with fresh straw and had a small drinking trough in the corner.

Mr. Soapstone carried Marvelous into her stall. He looked around at the other hogs. Then he straightened her ruff. "Perk up, girlie," he said.

Marvelous snorted. She looked terrible. Her head drooped so that her snout dragged in the straw. All around the other hogs were strutting in their stalls. Marvelous slunk over to the water trough. She lay down and buried her head under it.

"Get the smelling salts!" Mr. Soapstone said. "She may be dizzy from the ride."

An official came by to say the hog judging would begin in an hour. Mr. Soapstone held a bottle of smelling salts under Marvelous's snout. The other pigs were prancing in their stalls. Marvelous sneezed and lay still.

"See if you can find a doctor!" Mr. Soapstone cried.

A doctor came and examined Marvelous. "There's nothing wrong with her," he said.

"Nothing wrong!" yelled Mr. Soapstone. "What do you mean there's nothing wrong! Look at her!"

The doctor looked at Mr. Soapstone and went away.

A man came by to say the hogs would begin lining up in forty-five minutes. Mr. Soapstone stood Marvelous on her feet. She sat down. Then she lay down.

Mr. Soapstone squatted beside her. "Be reasonable, Marvelous," he said.

Marvelous sighed.

Mr. Soapstone shook her. His face was getting red. "This may be the most important event of your life!"

Marvelous rolled over.

"Some pigs would be darn proud to be here!"

Marvelous sighed.

"But don't let *that* worry you!" Mr. Soapstone was beginning to shout. "Go ahead and throw your life away on some cement fountain."

Marvelous blinked listlessly.

Several hog owners had stopped to listen.

"Don't worry about me!" Mr. Soapstone yelled. "Go your own way! Throw away your chances!"

Mrs. Soapstone tapped his shoulder. "I don't think

she can understand you, dear." Marvelous rolled over on her back. Her legs dangled pathetically.

"That's your decision, then?" Mr. Soapstone shouted. He looked in exasperation at the other hogs standing obediently in their stalls.

"All right!" he yelled at Mrs. Soapstone.

"All right what?" she said.

Mr. Soapstone jammed on his straw hat. "You go call that truck driver," he growled.

17

Lemon, Iris, and Mr. Soapstone waited at the entrance to the fairgrounds.

"Marvelous makes me *so* mad," Iris said.

"I knew she'd do this," said Lemon.

Mr. Soapstone paced back and forth, swearing. He kept looking at his watch. "Where is that fellow?" he growled.

"There he is!" Iris squealed. She pointed down the road.

On the horizon they could see a cloud of dust. An orange truck came hurtling toward them.

"This way!" Mr. Soapstone shouted, jumping onto the running board. Lemon and Iris scrambled into the back of the truck next to the dolphin. The truck shot toward the Hog Pavilion.

The other hogs and their owners were lined up, ready for the grand march past the judging stand. Mrs. Soapstone was standing at the entrance to the

Hog Pavilion, wringing her hands. "Oh, thank goodness!" she said as the truck pulled up. "She's getting worse. She keeps holding her breath and turning blue."

Lemon and Iris ran to get Marvelous. She was peeping out through the gate of her stall. As soon as she saw the girls, she flopped onto her back and held her breath.

"It's all right, Marvelous. He's here," Lemon cried.

"Come on," she said to Iris, "we'll have to carry her."

They couldn't lift Marvelous, so they dragged her.

"She's going to be a terrible mess," Iris said. "She'll look like she never had a bath or anything."

Lemon worried about the ruff. It was coming unpleated as they bumped along.

Mr. Soapstone and the man with the truck were hoisting the dolphin onto a dolly. "I never seen the likes of this," the trucker said.

All the hog owners were watching with interest. Their hogs stood obediently, waiting to march. Lemon and Iris tugged Marvelous around to the back of the truck. "Look, Marvelous!" Lemon said.

Marvelous wouldn't open her eyes.

"Look!" Lemon shouted.

With a last heave Mr. Soapstone and the man with the truck settled the dolphin on the dolly. Mr.

94

Soapstone turned to look at Marvelous. "Well?" he said.

"She won't open her eyes," said Lemon.

Mr. Soapstone strode over to Marvelous and set her on her feet. She blinked. Then all at once she squealed. It was a squeal of joy. It made everyone but Mr. Soapstone smile.

Marvelous came to life at once. She cavorted around the dolphin. She snorted. She grunted. The hog owners laughed. The other hogs looked startled.

Lemon and Iris caught her and straightened up her ruff. Mrs. Soapstone dusted her back with a clean handkerchief. "That pig seems almost like human," said the man with the truck.

"That's because she's a champion, of course," Lemon said.

Then all at once Lemon felt funny. The Soapstones were always saying Marvelous was a champion, but what did *that* mean? You had to win a ribbon to be a champion. That meant Marvelous had to win a ribbon, right here, right now. Otherwise she was just a pig.

Lemon looked around at the other pigs. They were *all* plump. They were *all* well brushed. Besides that, they were well behaved. Marvelous didn't look so special. Except for the way she was jumping around, she looked just like all the other pigs. "What if she doesn't win?" Lemon whispered to Iris.

Iris looked startled. "I never thought of that."

A voice came over the loud-speaker. "All hog owners prepare to march," it said. "The judging is about to begin."

"Line her up! Line her up!" Mr. Soapstone said nervously.

"You know, dear, she'll never march without the dolphin," said Mrs. Soapstone.

"Why do you think I've got the fool thing on a dolly?" Mr. Soapstone growled. "Lemon and Iris will have to pull it."

The gates to the judging ring swung open. The band struck up a march. The first hog entered the ring. The other hogs followed one by one until they were all circling the fence.

Lemon had butterflies in her stomach. "Come on, Marvelous," she whispered. Together she and Iris tugged the dolly. It began to roll. Mr. Soapstone steadied the dolphin. "Easy now," he said.

Lemon and Iris entered the ring. Marvelous capered beside them, running around to check the dolphin, first on one side, then on the other.

"Walk!" Lemon hissed. But Marvelous kept jumping around the dolphin. She was obviously having a wonderful time. The spectators laughed and whistled and waved at her.

"Grab her!" Lemon whispered to Iris.

"I can't! She won't hold still long enough!"

The hogs went a second time around the ring. Lemon and Iris and the dolphin straggled along at the end of the line. Marvelous hopped casually back and forth between them as if they were all going to a picnic. They passed the judging stand, and Lemon peeked shyly at the judges.

The next time Marvelous goes by, she decided, I'll grab her no matter what. But Marvelous kept out of the way. She hopped along near the dolphin's tail where neither Lemon nor Iris could reach her.

Marvelous came waltzing around again. Lemon dived and grabbed the ruff. It began unpleating in her hands, but she held on. Marvelous struggled. "Stop it!" Lemon whispered fiercely. "Behave yourself!"

The crowd whistled. The judges stared.

"Walk!" Lemon hissed. Marvelous stopped squirming. Lemon held tight to the ruff and Marvelous walked. All at once she walked perfectly! "Good girl!" Lemon whispered.

"Nice pig!" said Iris.

18

The pigs started a third time around the ring. The judges made notes on their clipboards. The band struck up "The Missouri Waltz."

Marvelous walked sedately, taking tiny steps. She swayed a little in time with the music. Occasionally she glanced at the dolphin and grunted gently as though she were trying to reassure him.

Lemon hoped the march wouldn't go on much longer. Her arms were aching. She glanced at the judges. They were talking together, now and then nodding toward a particular hog.

All at once the band stopped playing. It left off in the middle of a bar. A voice came over the loudspeaker. "Line up your hogs!" Lemon and Iris glanced around. The other hog owners were lining up their pigs in the center of the ring.

"Come on," Lemon whispered.

It was hard to turn the dolly. Iris shoved from behind. Lemon tugged. Slowly the dolly turned. They dragged it and Marvelous to the center of the ring. They lined up four abreast at the end of the line.

The judges moved slowly down the row of hogs. They stopped before each one. One judge looked into ears. A second checked teeth. The third judge poked each hog in various places with a bamboo stick.

"Hold tight to Marvelous," Iris whispered. "She won't like being poked."

Lemon held tight. The judges had reached the last pig before Marvelous. Lemon admired the way the hog stood quietly to be inspected. She hoped that Marvelous was noticing, too.

The judges made notes on their clipboards. "Thank you," they said. They moved on to Marvelous.

"Marvelous O'Hara Soapstone?" the judges asked.

"Yes, sir," said Iris.

All three judges stood before them. "This is a most unusual situation," one judge said.

Lemon and Iris nodded.

"We don't understand the purpose of this fish. We have never seen a fish at a hog judging."

"Well, you see, Marvelous and the dolphin are in love," said Iris.

The judges smiled. "Oh, yes?" said the first judge.

"Marvelous won't go anywhere without him," said Lemon.

"Really!" The judges seemed interested.

"If he weren't here, she'd just lie down and hold her breath," said Iris.

"I've never heard of anything like that," the first judge said. "That's unusual behavior for a pig."

"That's because she's a champ—" Iris began. Then she stopped.

"A what?" said the judge.

"A very unusual pig," said Lemon.

The judges nodded. They wrote on their clip-boards. "We'll have a look at this unusual pig," the second judge said.

The first judge looked into Marvelous's ear. Lemon knew it was spotless. The judge with the bamboo stick walked slowly around her. He poked her gently in the side. Marvelous quivered. Then he poked her other side. He tapped her hoof. Marvelous stood stiff as stone. Her eyes followed the judge, but Lemon couldn't tell what she was thinking.

"Maybe I ought to check her friend," said the judge with the stick. He laughed.

For a minute Lemon didn't know what he meant. And then it was too late. The judge reached over and poked the dolphin.

Marvelous jumped straight into the air. Her blue ruff dangled in Lemon's hand. She flew at the judge, snarling. The judge yelled, and hopped up and down. He hobbled away holding his ankle. Marvelous scuttled behind the dolly. The crowd roared.

"She bit me!" shouted the hopping judge. "That pig bit me!"

19

He shouldn't have poked the dolphin," said Iris. "I don't blame Marvelous," Lemon said. "It was a stupid thing for him to do."

"Why can't she just act like a pig?" Mr. Soapstone said. "Why, of all the pigs I might have bought, did I get one who falls in love with cement fountains and bites judges?"

They were standing beside Marvelous's stall waiting for the results of the judging. Mrs. Soapstone had gone to look at quilts. "You know very well Marvelous isn't going to win," she had said.

"You can't be sure," said Mr. Soapstone. "She showed gumption. Judges like that."

"I don't think judges like being bitten," said Mrs. Soapstone.

The other hog owners were minding their own business. They didn't talk to the Soapstones. That made Lemon mad. "Biting a judge isn't the worst thing there is," she said.

"Just about," said Mr. Soapstone gloomily.

Marvelous was curled up beside the dolphin taking a nap. Mr. Soapstone bought three bottles of Orange Crush. They sat on a bale of straw and drank them. Nobody felt like talking.

The other hog owners paced back and forth watching the judging stand. At last the judges came walking toward the Hog Pavilion carrying red and yellow and blue ribbons.

Lemon didn't want to watch. "Let's go for a walk," she said.

"Nope. We have to face the music," said Mr. Soapstone.

The judges took the biggest ribbon and walked to a stall at the far end of the pavilion. "First prize to Spot, Mr. Johnson's Poland China," they said.

The second prize went to a fat black hog. Lemon didn't watch after that. Mr. Soapstone sat slumped on the straw bale, looking at his feet. "Can't expect to win ribbons when you act like that," he muttered.

After they had awarded the last ribbon, the judges walked over to the Soapstones. One judge had a bandage around his ankle. "We're sorry your pig didn't win a ribbon," the first judge said. "It's nothing personal."

"No need to be sorry," said Mr. Soapstone. "She didn't deserve one."

"She's an interesting pig," said the second judge.

"An unusual pig," said the judge with the bandage. "But, of course, under the circumstances we couldn't give her a ribbon."

Mr. Soapstone shrugged. "I understand," he said. "Thanks all the same."

"Maybe next year," the first judge said.

Mr. Soapstone nodded.

After the judges left, Mr. Soapstone gave Lemon and Iris each a dollar. "Might as well go and enjoy the Fair," he said gloomily.

"What are you going to do?" Lemon asked.

"I think I'll go talk to a couple of hog dealers," said Mr. Soapstone.

"What's that?" said Iris.

"Men who buy and sell hogs."

Lemon and Iris looked at each other.

"You don't mean you might sell Marvelous?" Lemon said.

"I'd like to have a pig sometime that acted like a pig," Mr. Soapstone said wistfully.

"But you can't sell Marvelous!" Lemon said. "She's one of our family!"

"It would be like selling Mother!" Iris cried.

"No need to shout," said Mr. Soapstone. "Nothing's definite."

Lemon and Iris walked out of the Hog Pavilion. They walked past Spot, the champion hog. "I don't think that's such a good pig," Iris said.

Lemon looked at the blue ribbon hanging on Spot's stall. "So what?" she said. "The judges thought so."

They walked toward the midway. Lemon scuffed her sandals in the dust. "What if he sells her?" she said.

"I'll kill myself."

"Don't be stupid, Iris. I mean really, what if he does?"

"I'll find her. I'll go live where she is."

Lemon sniffed.

"Maybe nobody'll want her now she's not a champion any more," Iris said.

Lemon hadn't thought of that. "She's still a champion to me," she answered.

"But maybe not to people who buy pigs."

"Maybe not," Lemon said doubtfully. Somehow that didn't cheer her up much.

20

With a dollar apiece to spend, Lemon and Iris had lots of choices on the midway. They had two rides in the bumper cars. Then they each had a ride on the merry-go-round. "I'm getting too old for the merry-go-round," Iris said. "It used to be a lot more fun."

"Everything used to be a lot more fun," said Lemon.

"Cotton candy usually cheers me up," Iris said.

They bought two cones of cotton candy. It was blue. Every other year it had been pink. "I can't eat blue cotton candy," Iris said. "It's not right."

"Nothing's right," said Lemon. "I feel awful. I think I just want to go back and sit by Marvelous."

Iris nodded slowly. "Me too," she said. "I want to spend her last hours with her."

They turned and walked sadly back toward the Hog Pavilion. "I've never felt so awful at the Fair before, except the year I was getting chicken pox," Iris said.

Mrs. Soapstone was standing outside the Hog Pavilion holding a new quilt. "Where's your father?" she said.

"He's looking for someone to buy Marvelous," Lemon answered.

"But he can't sell Marvelous!" Mrs. Soapstone cried.

Lemon and Iris stared at their mother. "You want to *keep* Marvelous?" Iris said.

Mrs. Soapstone got red. "I'm used to her," she said.

"If you want to keep Marvelous, Daddy will never sell her!" Lemon said.

Iris jumped up and clapped her hands. "We've got to find him!" she shouted. "Let's go!"

They ran up and down the midway looking for their father. They ran past tents selling quilts and baked goods. They ran past a pickle judging, past a fortune teller, past a man selling chameleons and painted turtles. But they didn't see their father anywhere until they had run full circle back to the Hog Pavilion. And there he was, lifting Marvelous into the trailer.

"You didn't sell her!" Lemon cried.

"Never mind about that," said Mr. Soapstone. Marvelous's hoof was caught in Mrs. Chew's sign. "Push that hoof out, will you?"

Lemon got Marvelous's hoof untangled. She helped her father lift Marvelous into the trailer. "Mother wants to keep her, too," said Lemon. "She says you *can't* sell Marvelous."

Mr. Soapstone grunted. "Well, I didn't sell her, she'll be happy to learn."

Marvelous was glancing around nervously for the dolphin.

"See if you can find that fellow with the truck," Mr. Soapstone said. "Let's get that fish loaded before Marvelous has another fit."

Lemon found the man with the truck testing his strength at a booth on the midway. He didn't want to leave much. "I'm sorry," Lemon said, "but you know how Marvelous gets."

"Yeah, yeah," said the man. "Personally I don't think that pig's the only crazy one around here."

Mr. Soapstone and the trucker hoisted the dolphin back into the truck. Marvelous watched anxiously while Mr. Soapstone secured him with ropes.

Lemon thought the dolphin looked beautiful sitting in the truck with the sun sparkling on his cement tail. "I don't blame Marvelous at all," she whispered to Iris. "I'd bite somebody for poking him, too."

21

Going home, Mr. Soapstone stayed close behind the truck so that Marvelous could keep an eye on the dolphin. He was in a terrible mood.

"I'm glad you didn't sell her," Mrs. Soapstone said.

Mr. Soapstone grunted. "Who'd want a crazy pig like that?"

"You didn't even try to sell her, did you?" said Mrs. Soapstone. "You wanted to keep her, too."

"Never mind about that," Mr. Soapstone said gruffly.

"Well, didn't you?"

Mr. Soapstone groaned. "I guess I was the only one around here who really cared if Marvelous won first prize," he said.

Lemon and Iris smiled to themselves. They watched the dolphin's tail swaying in the truck ahead of them. "What burns me up," Mr. Soapstone said, "is she was obviously the best pig at the Fair. If it hadn't been for that two-bit ton of cement she'd have won."

"Now," said Mrs. Soapstone. "Now, now."

Mr. Soapstone grunted and frowned through the windshield.

The truck bounced over the rutted road. The Soapstones' car bounced after it. "I can't understand what she sees in that fish," Mr. Soapstone said. "His tail's all wrong for one thing."

Nobody answered. The sun was going down. Lemon yawned. She was getting sleepy.

"The dolphin looks alive swaying back and forth like that," Iris said. "Like he's swimming."

"Isn't he swaying an awful lot?" Lemon said.

"I believe he is!" Mrs. Soapstone cried.

"A rope must have broken!" Mr. Soapstone shouted. "Wouldn't you know it!" He honked at the truck.

The man in the truck stuck his head out of the cab. He nodded. He waved. Then he speeded up. "The fool thinks I mean to go faster!" Mr. Soapstone yelled. He honked again. He waved out the window. The man in the truck waved back and accelerated.

The dolphin's tail rocked back and forth like a pendulum. Mr. Soapstone kept honking and waving. He speeded up. They flew over the ruts. He yelled. The man in the truck kept going.

"That man must be crazy!" Mr. Soapstone cried.

Lemon and Iris bounced around the back seat.
Marvelous squealed in the trailer. Clouds of dust
rose behind the truck so that part of the time it was
invisible. Mr. Soapstone swore. "That fool's doing
seventy," he shouted.

The Soapstones' car tore after the truck. Once
in a while the dust blew away, and they could see
the dolphin lurching from side to side in the back.

Then all at once the truck hit a pothole. The dolphin bounced into the air. He rose above the clouds of dust. The Soapstones saw the last bit of rope break. The dolphin curved gracefully in an arc above the truck. For a moment he seemed to be flying. He seemed to be swimming in air. Then he turned nose down and headed for the ground.

Mr. Soapstone slammed on the brakes. Lemon and Iris screamed. The dolphin smashed into the ground nose first and collapsed into a pile of broken cement.

22

At first nobody said anything. They watched the truck rattle into the distance doing seventy miles an hour in a cloud of dust.

"Smashed to smithereens," Mr. Soapstone said finally.

Nobody else said a word.

Then from the trailer came a long, low howl. It went on and on and on. It sounded like January. "I've never heard a pig make a sound like that," said Mr. Soapstone.

He got out of the car and walked over to the pile of dolphin. Lemon and Iris ran around to comfort Marvelous. She was leaning out of the trailer looking at the dolphin. She howled. It's like wind in weather stripping, Lemon thought. It's the saddest sound I've ever heard.

"Not much left," Mr. Soapstone called.

Mrs. Soapstone got out of the car with her new quilt. "We'll take him home," she said.

Mr. and Mrs. Soapstone spread the quilt in the road. They filled it with the cement pieces. They dragged them in the quilt over to the trailer. "I don't see any use in this," Mr. Soapstone said, but he hoisted pieces one by one into the trailer anyway.

It took a long time. Marvelous had stopped howling. She sniffed each new piece and whimpered gently. She looked confused. Lemon was crying. "Maybe we could repair him," she said. "Maybe Iris and I could do it."

Nobody answered.

Mrs. Soapstone spread her quilt out in the trailer for Marvelous to rest on. Marvelous sat down on it. She put one hoof on part of the dolphin's tail. She stared straight ahead.

The Soapstones were quiet riding home. Mr. Soapstone drove slowly. Lemon and Iris watched Marvelous through the rear window. She never took her hoof from the dolphin's tail. She seemed to look straight at Lemon and Iris, but they could see she was thinking of something else.

The Soapstones drove into town as the sun was setting. Mrs. Chew's sign flapped sadly. Mr. Soapstone turned into the driveway and stopped the car. "Well, that's the worst Fair I ever went to," he said, "bar none."

Mrs. Soapstone went into the house to get supper. Lemon and Iris helped their father lead Marvelous to the sty. After that they helped him carry all the

pieces of the dolphin into the sty, too, because nobody could think what else to do with them.

Marvelous sat down in the midst of the cement
chunks. She rested her head on the dolphin's tail.
From time to time she whimpered. Lemon picked
her an early blooming chrysanthemum. Marvelous
ate it slowly, petal by petal, as though it didn't matter
whether she ate it or not.

"It looks like Pompeii out there," Mr. Soapstone
said at supper.

"I don't think that's funny," said Mrs. Soapstone.
She gave everyone a spoonful of peas. She gave
everyone an ear of corn. Then Marvelous began to
howl.

The Soapstones tried to eat their supper. Marvelous kept howling. Mrs. Soapstone asked if
anyone would like another lamb chop. Marvelous
howled. "This is terrible!" Mrs. Soapstone said.

Lemon and Iris helped their mother wash dishes.
Lemon turned the water on full blast. She clattered
plates. Iris sang. She banged pots. They could still
hear Marvelous perfectly.

"It's heartbreaking," said Mrs. Soapstone.

Lemon and Iris carried out the pail of slops. They
put it beside Marvelous so that she wouldn't have
to move. She stopped howling long enough to eat
a few peas.

The Soapstones sat on the screen porch, drinking

iced tea before bedtime. Marvelous was quiet. Sometimes she was quiet for as long as five minutes, and
they thought that she had fallen asleep. Then she
would begin howling again. "I hope she won't do
that all night," Mrs. Soapstone said. "I don't think
I could stand it."

Mr. Soapstone rattled his glass. In a way it was
worse when Marvelous wasn't howling because then
they were waiting for her to begin again. "Maybe we
ought to bury the dolphin," said Iris.

"He isn't dead," Mr. Soapstone said. "I mean he
wasn't alive—" Marvelous began to howl. "Oh,
damn!" Mr. Soapstone shouted. "I can't stand it!" He
slammed down his iced tea glass. He stood up.

"I'm glad to hear you say so," said a voice from
the honeysuckle bushes. "I was just thinking the
same thing myself."

Mrs. Chew came padding into the porch light. She
was wearing an old gray robe and pink-feather slippers. She was carrying a bucket of cement.

"In my opinion," she said, "that animal could be
patched up."

Mr. Soapstone looked at Mrs. Chew's bucket
doubtfully. Marvelous howled.

"Try it!" Mrs. Soapstone cried.

Mr. Soapstone shrugged. "I doubt it'll work," he
said.

"Fiddle," said Mrs. Chew. "You lift and I'll glue.

My grandfather, as you may know, was a sculptor."

"Iris and I can help!" Lemon said eagerly, but Mrs. Soapstone said it was their bedtime.

"Oh, naturally," Iris grumbled. "Just when the interesting part begins."

Lemon nudged her. "We can watch from upstairs."

Lemon and Iris leaned on their window sill and watched Mr. Soapstone turning on lights outside. He turned on the porch lights. He turned on the car lights. Mrs. Chew came climbing through the bushes with a bridge lamp on a long extension cord.

Marvelous stopped howling and blinked.

Mrs. Chew stirred cement with the handle of a broom. Mr. Soapstone hung a lantern on the fence and began sorting cement chunks into piles. Marvelous followed him back and forth, sniffing.

"I could easily watch all night," Iris said. Then she slid to the floor and fell asleep.

Lemon put her cheek on the window sill and tried to stay awake. Her father was carrying a chunk of cement to the center of the sty. He's nice, she thought. I wouldn't be so nice to someone I was mad at.

Mr. Soapstone dumped a shovelful of wet cement on the chunk. Mrs. Chew spread it out with a trowel. It's a big job, Lemon thought. It will take them hours. And then, although she hadn't intended to, Lemon flopped down beside Iris and fell asleep.

23

Iris woke first and shook Lemon. It was very early, barely daylight. They scrambled up from the floor and looked out the window. Mrs. Chew was spreading cement. Mr. Soapstone was holding the dolphin's tail in his arms.

"They fixed him!" Iris said happily.

The dolphin stood in the center of the sty with everything but his tail in place. He looked like himself. It was hard to tell he'd ever been broken.

Lemon and Iris ran out to the sty. Their mother was asleep with her head against the fence. Marvelous was standing beside the dolphin, keeping an eye on him.

"Well, what do you think?" Mr. Soapstone said.

"He's perfect!" said Lemon.

That wasn't quite true. The dolphin had looked better from a distance. Close up you could see that he was full of cracks. Cement had run down both his sides and his head tilted oddly. But Lemon didn't feel like saying so.

"Personally," Mr. Soapstone said, "I think he's better than he was before. I was pretty sure I could improve him."

"Hand me the tail," said Mrs. Chew.

They watched Mrs. Chew set the tail in place. She settled it carefully, then stood back to admire it.

"Perfect," Mr. Soapstone said. "A work of art."

Marvelous walked slowly around the dolphin. She rubbed her snout against his sides soothingly. Then she walked over and nuzzled Mrs. Chew.

"She's saying thank you," Iris said.

Mrs. Chew just coughed and straightened her hat, but anyone could tell she was pleased.

Mr. Soapstone stood back and looked at the dolphin. "Darn nice looking fish," he said. "Wake up your mother."

Mrs. Soapstone was embarrassed. "I don't know how I happened to fall asleep," she said.

"What do you think of him?" said Mr. Soapstone.

"Why, he's wonderful!" said Mrs. Soapstone. She walked all around, studying the dolphin. Then she invited Mrs. Chew to have breakfast.

"Better get Marvelous her slops," said Mr. Soapstone. "She stayed up all night long watching."

Marvelous looked tired, but she looked happy. Lemon gave her an extra helping of roses with her

breakfast. Marvelous fell asleep with her chin in the slops trough.

At breakfast Mr. Soapstone lifted his orange juice glass. "I propose a toast to Marvelous and the dolphin," he said.

Lemon and Iris stared.

"But you don't even like the dolphin!" Lemon said.

"And aren't you mad at Marvelous?" said Iris.

"The dolphin has improved greatly," Mr. Soapstone said. "And I guess it's no use being mad at Marvelous. If she wants to throw away her life on a cement fish, it's her business. Batty, of course, but her business."

He sipped his orange juice and looked out the window. "I suppose not everyone *wants* to be a champion," he said thoughtfully.

"Personally," said Mrs. Chew, "I've never cared much for blue-ribbon champions. There are other kinds I like better."

"There aren't any other kinds," Iris said.

"Yes there are," said Lemon. She knew what Mrs. Chew meant for once. "You don't have to win a blue ribbon to be something special," she said.

Mrs. Chew nodded. She nodded so hard her sun hat fell into the marmalade.

Lemon helped her clean the brim. She was beginning not to mind Mrs. Chew so much. She supposed that if Mrs. Chew wanted to be crazy, that was her business.

Mrs. Soapstone got up to pour coffee. The telephone rang, and Iris ran to answer it. "Somebody wants to come see Marvelous," Iris called. "They say they read about her in the paper."

"What?" said Mr. Soapstone.

Before Iris could answer him, the doorbell rang. The telephone rang again. Someone began knocking at the back porch door.

Mrs. Soapstone put down the coffee pot and ran to the window. "The driveway's full of people!" she cried.

Lemon looked out. It was true. Whole families were standing in the Soapstones' driveway, pointing to the sty and looking excited. People were lining the sidewalk. The back yard was filling up.

Iris ran to answer the door. Then the telephone rang. "What on earth is happening?" Mrs. Soapstone cried.

Mr. Soapstone came stamping into the kitchen. He waved a newspaper under her nose. "This!" he shouted.

24

Mr. Soapstone spread the newspaper on the kitchen table. For a moment the telephone and the doorbell rang and nobody paid any attention. All the Soapstones stared. On the front page of the paper was a picture of Marvelous. Underneath was the headline, PIG BITES JUDGE. And, under that, a smaller headline, *Unusual Love Story at County Fair*.

Mr. Soapstone sat down on the kitchen stool and folded his arms. "A man should be permitted to suffer disgrace with a little dignity," he said.

"Someone to see Marvelous!" Iris yelled from the front door.

"Send him around to the back yard, dear!" Mrs. Soapstone cried as the telephone began to ring again.

All at once the back door flew open. Mr. Hack clattered in. His eyes were popping. Behind him came a man with a microphone on a long cord. "What's going on!" shouted Mr. Soapstone. "Can't a man have peace in his own kitchen!"

"He followed me in," said Mr. Hack.

"Are you the owner?" said the man with the microphone.

"I am L. L. Soapstone," Mr. Soapstone said.

"Folks, I'm standing here in the Soapstones' kitchen—"

"Oh, good grief!" cried Mrs. Soapstone. "We're on the radio!"

"And standing beside me is the owner of that pig we've all been reading about. Mr. Soapstone, can you tell us a little about your pig and her cement friend?"

Mr. Soapstone looked as if he'd been struck by lightning. He shook his head and glared at the radio announcer.

"I'm going to ask Mr. Soapstone to give us his version of this remarkable love story," the announcer said.

Mr. Soapstone began pacing the kitchen floor, swearing under his breath. The announcer followed him back and forth, trailing the microphone cord.

"Can you tell us how they met?" he said, thrusting the microphone under Mr. Soapstone's nose.

"Accidentally," Mr. Soapstone growled.

"And they've been inseparable ever since?"

"They have," said Mr. Soapstone.

"It must be difficult, moving that big cement fish from place to place."

"It takes planning."

"But you do it for Marvelous. Right, Mr. Soapstone?"

"That's right!" Lemon said before she could stop herself. "And even when she bit the judge and didn't win and Daddy was mad, he didn't sell her!"

The radio announcer bent down and held the microphone for Lemon.

"And," Lemon said, because now she couldn't stop at all, "when the dolphin fell off the truck and got smashed, our father stayed up all night patching him together."

"Your father and Mrs. Adelaide Chew," Mrs. Chew said loudly from the breakfast table.

"It sounds like your father's quite a hero around here," the announcer said.

"Oh, yes!" said Lemon. "Maybe some people think the things he does for Marvelous are a big joke, but we think it's wonderful."

Mr. Soapstone was staring curiously at Lemon and the radio announcer.

"You must be pretty proud to have a father who cares more about his pig's feelings than he does about winning blue ribbons," the announcer said.

Iris came nudging up to the microphone.

"We certainly are," she said loudly. "We think he's a champion."

Mr. Soapstone blushed and looked at his shoes. Everyone in the kitchen was staring at him. The announcer held out the microphone. "Do you want to say something, sir?" he asked.

Mr. Soapstone coughed. He straightened his shoulders and cleared his throat. "Some pigs like winning blue ribbons," he said into the microphone. "Some don't. I believe the choice should be left up to the pig." Then he shook the announcer's hand and bowed to everyone in the kitchen.

Mr. Hack was leaning against the refrigerator gazing at Mr. Soapstone. "Wow!" he said.

Mrs. Soapstone dabbed at her eyes with a handkerchief. Lemon and Iris grinned.

"Exactly the kind of speech my grandfather would have made," Mrs. Chew said. "Highly appropriate."

After a while they all went out onto the back porch. Mr. Soapstone waved to the crowd around the sty. Several people wanted his autograph.

Lemon and Iris set up a lemonade stand next to the rose bed. Mrs. Chew made a large painting of a finger that pointed toward the back yard to save Mrs. Soapstone's having to answer the door every five minutes. Mr. Soapstone stood at the kitchen window and watched the crowd.

People kept coming all afternoon. They bought

lemonade and stood around the sty with their cameras. Marvelous posed politely whenever anyone wanted her picture.

At five o'clock Lemon and Iris closed the stand and counted the money. They had $2.63. "Tomorrow," said Mr. Soapstone, "We'll build a ticket booth."

Iris picked up paper cups around the sty. Lemon filled the slops pail. The sun went down. The crickets whirred. Marvelous grunted peacefully.

The Soapstones were tired. They went to bed early. Marvelous curled up by the dolphin and fell asleep. The moon rose slowly over the ridgepole and shone down all night on the dolphin's cement tail.